F I R S T  S T O R Y

First Story aims to celebrate and foster creativity, literacy and talent in young people. We're cheerleaders for books, stories, reading and writing. We've seen how creative writing can build students' self-esteem and self-confidence.

First Story places acclaimed authors as writers-in-residence in state schools across the country. Each author leads weekly after-school workshops for up to sixteen students. We publish the students' work in anthologies and arrange public readings and book launches at which the students can read aloud to friends, families and teachers.

For more information and details of how to donate to First Story, see www.firststory.co.uk or contact us at info@firststory.co.uk.

Raising the Bar
ISBN 978-0-85748-041-5
Published by First Story Limited
www.firststory.co.uk
First Story
4 More London Riverside
London
SE1 2AU

Designer: Tony O'Keefe
Cover design: Tony O'Keefe
Printed in the UK by Intype Libra Ltd

First Story Limited is a registered charity number 1122939 and a private company limited by guarantee incorporated in England with number 06487410. First Story is a business name of First Story Limited.

Raising the Bar

An Anthology

BY THE FIRST STORY GROUP
AT CHENEY PLUS

EDITED AND INTRODUCED BY ALAN BUCKLEY | 2012

FIRST STORY

Fostering creativity, literacy and talent

Contents

Thank you

Kate Kunac-Tabinor and all the designers at OUP for their overwhelming support for First Story and **Tony O'Keefe** specifically for giving his time in designing this anthology.

Melanie Curtis at Avon DataSet for her overwhelming support for First Story and for giving her time in typesetting this anthology.

Anne Clark for her meticulous copy-editing.

The Staples Trust, Suzanne Brais and Stefan Green for their support of First Story in this school.

HRH the Duchess of Cornwall for her generous Patronage of First Story.

The Trustees of First Story:
Beth Colocci, Charlotte Hogg, Rob Ind, Andrea Minton Beddoes, John Rendel, Alastair Ruxton, David Stephens, Sue Horner and James Wood.

The Advisory Board of First Story:
Andrew Adonis, Julian Barnes, Jamie Byng, Alex Clark, Julia Cleverdon, Andrew Cowan, Jonathan Dimbleby, Mark Haddon, Josephine Hart, Simon Jenkins, Andrew Kidd, Rona Kiley, Chris Patten, Kevin Prunty, Deborah Rogers, Zadie Smith, William Waldegrave, and Brett Wigdortz.

Thanks to:
Jane and Peter Aitken, Ed Baden-Powell, Laura Barber, The Blue Door Foundation, Josie Cameron-Ashcroft, Anthony Clake, Molly Dallas, The Danego Charitable Trust, Peter and Genevieve Davies, Martin Fiennes, the First Story Events Committee, the First Story First Edition Club, Alex Fry, The Funding Network, Goldman Sachs Gives, Kate Harris, Kate Kunac-Tabinor, the John R. Murray Charitable Trust, Old Possums Trust, Oxford University Press, Philip Pullman, Pitt Rivers Museum, Quercus Books, Radley College, the Sigrid Rausing Trust, Clare Reihill, The Royal Society of Literature, Chris Smith, The Staples Trust, Teach First, Betsy Tobin, Richard Tresidder, Walker Books and Hannah Westland.

Most importantly we would like to thank the students, teachers and writers who have worked so hard to make First Story a success this year.

Foreword

Vic Moore, Susie Lopez and Justin Heenan – Cheney Plus Team

It is true to say that we debated running a First Story group in Cheney Plus for quite some time. We eventually decided to go ahead, but not without a small amount of trepidation and our fingers firmly crossed. Right from the start we got very lucky and realised we had worried for nothing. We got Alan Buckley. From their very first meeting, the students took to Alan and from the first lesson they started to engage in their exploration of poetry with him. Friday mornings became a favourite for staff and students, reading and writing poetry fuelled with treats of biscuits, cakes and doughnuts. Our students have amazed us by producing outstanding work ranging from sad and deeply insightful poems to verses that were wonderfully silly and fun. They have chosen the title, organised the design and 'look' of the book. This really and truly is their creation and they all have every reason to be immensely proud of it. It has been a privilege and a pleasure to be able to help them along the journey.

Introduction

Alan Buckley

In July 2011 I joined a morning trip for Cheney Plus students to Oxford Ice Rink. Vic Moore and Susie Lopez (the members of staff involved with the First Story project) and I had agreed it would be a good way to start getting to know the students, before we began the workshops with them in September. I also felt it would be a fair exchange. I hadn't been ice skating for years, and had never been any good at it – given that I was going to ask them to do something that was exposing, and where they might feel they risked making fools of themselves, I felt it was only right that I did something similar first.

As it turned out, although I couldn't match the students' speed and skilfulness, I didn't fall over – and, when it came to writing, neither did they. None of the group was older than fifteen, and only one had previously done any creative writing. While it's true that the sessions didn't always run smoothly (I'm indebted to Susie and Vic for their tireless work in the classroom both to maintain order, and to support individual students with their writing), most weeks there would be a miraculous period of about ten minutes when all that could be heard was the scratching of pens on paper. Increasingly, students took risks in their poems, as they wrote about the impacts of loss and bereavements, their desire for love, connection and belonging, and – in many cases – their fear of growing up and having to face the world. At the same time, a number of students found ways to express their (often surreal) sense of humour through their poems, and while there's a real rawness to the writing here, there's a great sense of vitality too.

Cheney Plus is an inclusion project within the grounds of Cheney School, one of the largest secondary schools in Oxford; it works with young people who can't manage being in mainstream education, or whose behaviour puts them at risk of exclusion from regular schools. Inevitably, its students feel different, and that they are to some degree looked down on by the rest of the school. We chose the title "Raising the Bar" for two reasons. As a phrase it suggests a heightening of what is thought possible – not only had students' expectations of themselves been raised by telling them they were going to write a book, but the expectations of others around what Cheney Plus students could achieve were also being positively challenged. The phrase has a second meaning, of course. For students who have, for whatever reason, been barred from the mainstream, this book is a way of removing – however briefly – the division between them and the rest of Cheney, by showing that they can write as directly and powerfully as their peers in the main school.

I'd like to thank Vic, and Susie in particular, for all the time and effort they've put in both within and between sessions to make this project a success. Just as importantly, my thanks go to all the students who've been part of the group, and who've been willing to take a step outside of what they thought they could do. You have a book to be proud of.

If I Look in the Mirror, I Don't Even Recognise Myself

(after "Signs" by *Gillian Wearing*)

I want to go back to 1976
I want to go back in time
        and change my life style

To start my life again

Take away the things that make me worry
Make people share who they are inside
Shut out all the bad things in life

To start my life again

Help people who need help in the world
Stop all the robbing and killings in the world
Make the world a better place to live in

To start my life again

I wish I had the chance to meet my parents
        and to make them proud
I want my Nan to still be alive

To start my life again

Can't help you climb your ladder
I'm busy climbing mine
That's how it's been
since the dawn of time

To start my life again.

The Cheney Plus Group

Half Term

Home all day
And I'm bored
Lying in bed all day
Flicking thru the TV channels
There's nothing on
Everything is boring
Running out of time
Midnight already.

Ryan

Girls

Gobby Girls talk all the time
Immature all day
Rude to boys all day
Lippy going on all day
Stubborn views all the time.

Tyron

Bike

Riding my bike on the pavement.
Doing no-handed down the road,
and nearly knocking someone over,
because I can make rollies on my bike.

Lewis

Dream House

It's a place to chill out and have fun,
you can party, play darts, have drinks,
even bring your mates along.
There's four bedrooms with double beds
for the end of the night.
It's got an Xbox 360,
PS3, laptop, 32-inch TV,
a dog, a cat, a fish, a snake, a lizard.
This is my dream.
This is what I would have
if I won the lottery.
It's the biggest dream I could ever have.

Dylan

I Remember

I remember when I fell down the stairs with a bin on my head.

I remember smacking my brother and my dad telling me off.

I remember moving house to go live with my nan.

I remember choking on a sweet for the first time.

I remember standing on the beige stairs in my temporary house.

I remember rolling on an ants' nest.

I remember eating a bug beetle.

I remember laughing at *Moo, moo, dead*.

I remember getting drunk for the first time when I was five years old at my auntie's wedding, and throwing up on my bridesmaid's dress.

I remember throwing a glass bottle at my sister.

I remember letting myself out of the house when I was two years old, and walking to my sister's school and hugging her.

I remember laughing at little ladies.

I remember reading my first book with no mistakes.

I remember plaiting my mum's hair and doing her make-up.

I remember hitting my uncle because he said I had brown eyes.

I remember giving my dad a tattoo.

Addie

You Are

You are like a rainy miserable day
You are like a stormy sea
You are like a boat sinking into the deep black sea
You are like a broken record that's really annoying.

Adam

No Regrets

I know I ran away
when I was overcrowded
in my head.

But inside
I don't regret it.

Kimmie

Fear

Fear of seeing police in the rear-view mirror.
Fear of seeing the speed camera.
Fear of seeing the 30 mph sign.
Fear of the breathalyser.
Fear of the lights turning red.
Fear of the icy roads.
Fear of the brakes not working.
Fear of someone stepping out in the road.
Fear of death.

Mathew

My Head

Is a pillow full of dreams!!!
Is the wardrobe from Narnia,
    because it's full of imagination and it never ends.
Is a glass of water that's neither half empty nor half full.
Is a bomb full of explosive.
Is a firework exploding with imagination and thoughts.
Is a fossil full of bones and memories.

Kai

A Luxury Let-down

Not so funny
On his own
Entirely random
Luxury Comedy was a let-down
Fully disappointing
In every way
Even as a fan I thought this show was a pile
Lost his style
Don't know why
Is it time
No it's money
Gone but not forgotten (The Mighty Boosh).

Tom

Lipstick

I sit in the make-up bag waiting to be used,
covered in eyeliner sharpenings
and opened tops of mascaras.

I don't want to be red,
or plum, or purple.
I like being bright pink.

I wait for a hand to reach down
into the make-up bag
and pick me up.

When I get picked out I become shiny
and glossy, but start to wear out
at the same time.

Then I wind back down,
and my lid goes back on top,
and I'm thrown back in the bag,

ready for next time.

Alice

Locket

I am a gold locket.
I am the shape of a heart.
I have a picture of her nan.
I feel like I'm going to get lost in a dark room,
but I know I won't get lost.
I will always be on Kim's warm neck.

Kimmie

Being a Dog

I'm hot, can you turn the heating off?
You don't have to wear a fur coat.

I can hear what you're saying,
and . . . I don't mean for my hair to fall out.

You want me to walk – what, now!
No – can't be bothered.

I know I'm lying on the radiator,
but you can all see me here.

OK I'll walk – get the lead and treats.
Park and back – OK.

Reprieve – Match of the Day has started.
Back to sleep . . .

Vic

Self-portrait

Funny
Interesting
Grabbing
Hurtful
Taunting
Important
Nasty
Gagging.

Tyron

I Remember

I remember waking up one day and running to the door as I heard the post being delivered. It was the paperwork for my bike; it was finally here after six weeks. I was so happy because it meant I could ride it for the first time. It was great, the wind in my helmet; it was a great ride, but then the problems started.

It was dying slowly, so I got it home and took it all apart and put it in my bedroom. Then I bought new fuel filters and a new exhaust; I put the new parts on but it would not start. The fuel and air mixture was wrong. Then there was a small fire, so I ran to the hosepipe and turned it on and put the fire out.

It was a disaster, but I persevered, and it is with us today, all fixed up and running well. I have put all new parts on it, new carburettor, fuel filter, new air filter, new exhaust. I remember the time it died and I brought it back once again; I remember.

Mathew

You Are

You are nice and helpful
You are full of joy

You are full of happiness
You are full of laughter

You are full of movement
You are full of love

You are like a cheetah
You are fast as lightning

You are soft as a sofa
You are the best.

Lewis

House

My house, my house.
I hate my house.
It's scary, haunted.
I always hear noises
like there's ghosts.

They may be there to scare.
They may be there to help.
I don't know!
I hope it's my nan, someone
in my family. They may be in heaven
but they're still there.

Tyron

Home

Home is a peaceful place,
but there is nowhere to run.
Also no one around.
It is a safe place.
No one to talk to.
Also, no love in my life,
but just nice people.
Just a mouse crawling in a small hole.
Also a loud studio in the cellar,
and me tucked in a corner.

Kimmie

[Woof woof woof bark. Sneeze sniffle "Chaos" – *translation into English: This poem is spoken in Dog, not English. This poem is called "Chaos"*]

Chaos

Woof woof woof sneeze
Woof woof woof woof woof
Sniffle sneeze woof woof woof
BARK

[Woof Chaos – *translation into English by Chaos the dog*]

Kai

Fear

Fear of getting shot.
Fear of drowning.
Fear of being disabled.
Fear of tarantulas.
Fear of writing.
Fear of getting stabbed.
Fear of rats.
Fear of the dead.
Fear of Vic.
Fear of small spaces.
Fear of my sister.
Fear of heights.
Fear of fire.

Adam

You Are

You are a monkey,
        cheeky and funny
You are a Carlsberg,
        sour and strong
You are a burger,
        fat and nice
You are a Mini,
        small and round.

Tyron

Home

When all has been said and done,
what really counts is to get
someone to call you at five to talk.

I really want my room to be how I choose
and have everything I've always wanted,
and have a dream house of my own.

Stacey

My Head

Is a bottle of Cola
Is a bath full of water
Is a freezer, cold and icy
Is a pillow full of dreams.

Ryan

Gift

Strength and protection you hand me
in times of my high emotion.

Life is something you gave to me
showing love and devotion.

There is no gift I can give you
that would repay all you have given to me.

But know that I am your proud daughter
and my love you can guarantee.

Kimmie

Rhinoceros

The alien spaceship landed in Cheney School just after 11 o'clock. Suddenly a green alien came out fast and said *Hello*. He went into a shop and bought some sweets. He left the shop and got into his Ford Mustang and revved his big V8 at 12,000 rpm. *Oi, you!* shouted the old lady, *Stop revving that stupid car. Drive on or get out! You should get a Prius – much better for the environment* she said. So she went home to meet a man called Hippo. I said *It's going down like it's meant to; it's not nine but it's ten to. Ten to nine, and it's time to go to the zoo*. So I went to the zoo to see a rhinoceros, and its name was Susie!

The Cheney Plus Group

Dream Home

My dream home is my garage
where I will have tools, cars,
and it is a space where I can spend
all day and all night
working on anything and everything
I can get my hands on.

I will have lights and tools
all over the garage
and I will eat and sleep
in my garage. My garage is my home:
my home is special to me
because it is my life,

and if I did not have this
I would not be here today.
I will have all snap-on tools,
car ramps and pictures of cars and bikes.
My garage will have the highest security
so no one can get in but me.

My garage is my life and I love it
and I will not change anything
about my life.

Mathew

I Remember

I remember when my great nan
was alive she was the best nan
you could ever get, she was amazing.

I remember when I was younger
I got my mum's phone and put it
in a bucket of water.

I remember when I was about three
and my sister was a baby.
She was pissing me off
so I stabbed her in the back
with scissors. I felt really bad.

Tyron

The Stories I Read From My Body

The mark below my right thumb
is where my sister was pretending to cut me,
but the knife slipped. She's crazy!

The mark on my right forearm
is where my sister burnt me
with hair straighteners.

The two dots on my left forearm
are where I stabbed myself with a pencil.
The pencil lead's still under my skin.

The scar near to my left elbow
is where I got kicked into a wall.

The scar just under my hairline
is where I fell off a swing
and hit my head on concrete.

The round mark on my leg
is where Lewis chucked a rock at it.
I can stick a pencil in it
and it still doesn't hurt.

Adam

You Are

You are a penguin
You are a Fosters
You are a Mini
You are a muffin
You are a cottage
You are a rose
You are sunshine.

Ryan

My Wacky Mother

You're my wacky mother
I'm your zany daughter.
We have a tie between us
that can't be undone.

We drive each other crazy
but we love each other too
and throughout I'll be sending
love to you.

Kimmie

The Pig

I have a grandmother called Olive.
She's very old-fashioned.
She wears big hats;
she doesn't take crap;
get on her nerves
and you're taking a slap.

She took me to a farm
and we saw a pig.
It then did a shit
so my nan picked up a stick
and hit it on its hip.

The story I'm telling you is true;
that's something Olive did do.

I stood there laughing until I cried.
After that I had sore eyes.

Amare

Fear

Fear of spiders.
Fear of ugly spiders' faces.
Fear of spiders going in my fucking mouth.
Fear of being bald.

Lewis

Achilles' Heel

Gets me up
And brings me down
Not the cure
Just the easy option
And my biggest problem.

Anon

CCTV

It's 12.52 pm.
It's raining and cold.
It's really busy this afternoon.
There is one child all alone, crying . . .
she's about two to three years old,
blonde hair, dark eyes,
about two and a half feet tall,
ears pierced, and she's wearing
Huggies, white and pink stripy socks,
she has a teddy and a light blue Teletubbies top.
The child has been wailing here
for an hour now.
She is crying and no one has come
to see if she's all right. It looks like
she isn't with anyone.

Addie

CCTV

It was 12 noon on a sunny Friday afternoon. There was an Aston Martin DB9 with a 6.2 litre V12. It was driving down towards Tesco's where it got stuck behind a bus. The Aston Martin went around the bus fast and hit . . . a Ford Mustang GT500 with a 7.2 litre V8 that was coming the other way. The driver of the Mustang was killed by the head-on collision. The driver of the Mustang had his foot flat to the floor on the accelerator, the rear wheels were smoking and spinning out of control.

A crowd of people started running towards the collision, and someone called 999. Meanwhile, the traffic was building up, and the police came towards Tesco's, weaving in and out of the cars to get to the site of the collision, followed by an ambulance and a fire engine. The police were going around the witnesses to see what happened, and the ambulance people went to the driver of the Aston Martin to see if he was OK. The fire brigade went to the Mustang to try and stop the wheels spinning out of control. They tried to stop them, then the RAC Recovery came to tow the Mustang and the Aston Martin away to the garage, to get the cars fixed and send them on their way on the road once again.

Mathew

Dream House

I want a house full of Chihuahuas
I want my house to have a candyfloss maker
I want a house with a spray-tan room and sunbeds
I want a house like Charlie and the Chocolate Factory.

Alice

You Are

You are like a beautiful flower fluttering in the wind
You are like the beating in my heart
You are like a cocktail on a special occasion
You are midnight (in other words like partying)
You are like a Nissan Skyline – beautiful.

Dylan

I Remember

I remember when I had to say goodbye
Our memories are still alive in my head and sky
I never wanted to say goodbye
I may only see you once a week
You need to stay strong not weak
Some lose, some succeed
Say something about my mum, you'll be bleeding
Make a wish list the number one thing
You'll be begging for my forgiveness
Don't try to mess with me coz I'm hot in the game
When I'm done you won't be the same!
The problem is you're at me like Aladdin
Got the genie in the bottle and I ain't even gassin'!

Kai

Susie

Sweet
Unselfish
Scary
Important
Energetic

Loopy
Outspoken
Pretty
'Elpful
Zany.

Stacey

Valentine

There's no denying that I fancy you.
You're fab and fun and fit.
I want you to be my Valentine
and I must admit
that I'd love to have you kiss me
and give me a cuddle too.
Say you'll be my Valentine
and make this dream come true.

Kimmie

Jungle Story

Once upon a time in the jungle, there was a young gorilla called Johnny. He fell in love with a fish called Masue. Masue was a gorgeous goldfish with sparkly dark grey eyes. Johnny was tall, hairy and handsome. He went down to the pond and as he looked down at his reflection he saw Masue. She smiled at him and their eyes became hearts.

A big heron ruined the moment and grabbed Masue with his big beak. Johnny pounded his chest and made a loud, deep cry. He ran as fast as he could; he ran to his friend's nest. "MR EAGLE HELP PLEASE, SOME HERON HAS TAKEN MASUE".

The eagle flew up and saw the heron. The eagle attacked the heron and grabbed Masue. He took her back to the pond, and Johnny ran down to the pond in tears. Masue was badly injured but she would be all right.

They fell in love and had their babies – they were tall, with hair on their heads, with tiny feet and hands; they were called humans.

Addie

Army Cadets

Thank you for coming.
We would like to take you on a five-day trip.
I will get you running and training.
I will push you to the limit.
I will make you run and do press-ups.
I want you smart in your uniform
AND ON TIME.

Lewis

School Jumper

My favourite place
is on the roof and J Block.
I tell him where to go.
I like the heat of fires
and the smell of smoke.
And I like the sound of his voice,
so I tell him to talk.
I don't like sports,
so I make him stand on the side.
I like lots of water,
so I make him flood the toilets.

Ryan

Fear

Fear of heights.
Fear of not waking up.
Fear of plane crashes.
Fear of drowning.
Fear of growing up.
Fear of crying, not laughing.
Fear of lizards.
Fear of trains.
Fear of fire.
Fear of sharks.
Fear of lions.
Fear of snakes.
Fear of some spiders.
Fear of graveyards.
Fear of blood.
Fear of seeing someone badly hurt.
Fear of scaffolding.
Fear of ladders.
Fear of hammers.
Fear of choking.
Fear of being in a small space.
Fear of J Block emails.
Fear of a misfire on the range.

Dylan

Dream Home

My ideal home would have
a giant speaker
inside the door,
and when girls
walk through the door
it blows their clothes off.

Kai

Home

I want a home
alone on a beach.
No tax or insurance,
no bills to pay.
Me and my woman
for the rest of my days.

Tom

You Are

You are a clown, you make us laugh
You are a monkey, cheeky
You are a banger racer, getting broke
You are a Pot Noodle
You are a fizzy pop, Dr P
You are School of Rock, Turkey Sub
You are the solar system
You are lunchtime, getting up
You are now the biggest in the house.

Vic

Special Day (For My Mother)

Some things work together;
some things are meant to be.
Some people are meant for each other,
and it's obvious to see
that you were made for one another,
we cannot imagine you apart.
May this day bring you a happiness
that forever fills your hearts.

Kimmie

To My Nan

I'm not sorry for stealing
your biscuits because
they were so nice.

But I'm sorry.
Please forgive me.
I didn't mean to push you.

I was angry. I didn't know
what I was doing. It's wrong.
Forgive me.

Tyron

Three Little Dots

I gave my dad a tiny tattoo on his finger
when he was asleep on the downstairs sofa.

I don't remember how old I was,
but I know I was young.

I used a sewing pin,
and ink out of a pen.

He woke up in shock
when the needle went through his finger,
then I poured the ink onto his hand.

He walked to the kitchen sink
and washed his hand.

He came back into the living room
and said *That was naughty,*
you shouldn't do it again.

Addie

Half Term

Having Fun
Annoying parents
Laughing with mates
Fighting
Talking
Energetic
Racing
My break.

Stacey

Four-letter Words (Don't Wait Just Read)

(after *Matthew Welton*)

Hair does look good
Matt will love cars
Kai's wish will come true
Kai's been with girl
          like lion want kill
It'll wait till noon

Been goin' down here
Need some beer soon
Back here we'll kill – Adam!
Who's like some wish
          that won't come true?
Tick tock tick tock
Your life goes bang

Alan does this shit
We're here each week
Ride your bike
Don't hi(t)ch hike
Come read this poem
It'll keep goin'

Don't wait just read.

Kai, Mathew, Vic & Alice

Fear

Fear of aeroplanes.
Fear of growing up.
Fear of dying.
Fear of first day of school.
Fear of not getting a job.
Fear of never seeing my mum.

Ryan

Ode to Ryan Eeley

Ryan, you make us crack up.
We miss you making us laugh.
We miss having your jokes and tricks.

Some of us are sad
we haven't got to meet you yet.

Ryan, your bad hair days are funny,
when you put your hood up.
We remember how you looked
that morning after the night before,
shaking and white as a sheet.

We miss the Ryan and Susie show.
If we made a sitcom
it would be like Little Britain,
with you and Susie as the Odd Couple.

We miss you cooking with chilli.
We miss cooking with washing-up liquid
and spitting in the soup.

Ryan, sometimes we don't understand you.
You are so annoying!
Sometimes you make us mad.

J Block will miss you.
As Vic says, in the words of The Drifters,
we see you "up on the roof".
We miss getting into trouble with you.

The Cheney Plus Group

My Head

Is a safe full of cash
Is a bus full of old people
Is a freezer full of ice cream
Is a broken record
Is a purse full of loose change
Is a computer with a record of love.

Kimmie

This is Just to Say

I have eaten the full English breakfast
that was on the table.

It was so hot but so good
the bacon just melted in my mouth.

Forgive me,
but I will have the same again
tomorrow,
same time, same place.

Thanks.
Forgive me,
but it was so good.

Mathew

The Authors

Adam Marshall – If Adam was an animal he'd be a terrier – he may be small, but he's very capable of getting your attention! Although Adam found being in the group with the older students a challenge, we still got some fine pieces of writing from him. Talk to him one-to-one and you'll realise both how thoughtful he can be, and what a dark sense of humour he has.

Addie Graham – If Addie was a cartoon character she'd be the rabbit from the Duracell adverts – because when it comes to writing she just keeps on going, long after everyone else has stopped. She may appear quiet on the surface but there's a real determination underneath that. She was particularly good at turning her childhood memories into startling poems.

Alice Morris – If Alice was a superhero she'd be Cat Woman, because she's glamorous and would give you a karate chop if you got out of hand. If she was an animal, she'd be a Chihuahua – underneath all the noise we suspect she's really quite friendly. Alice is fiery, funny and has the brightest pink fingernails in the whole school; and we all loved her "Lipstick" poem.

Dylan Fiddes – If Dylan was a colour he'd be orange, because yellow is safe and nice and red is dangerous; if he was a dog he'd be a Husky, because they're beautiful and really hard to control. We haven't seen as much of Dylan as we'd have liked, but he showed his talents early on with a poem written to persuade a girl to go out with him – though we're not sure how well it worked . . .

Kai Sawyer – If Kai was a superhero he'd be the Silver Surfer, because he clearly lives partly in hyperspace; whatever you're thinking, Kai's already got there before you. As he says in one of his own poems, his head "is a firework exploding with imagination and thoughts", but he also has a wonderfully off-the-wall sense of humour, and is the only student at Cheney Plus to be fluent in Dog as well as English.

Kimmie Hughes – If Kimmie was an animal she'd be a kangaroo, because she likes jumping around the place; if she was a fictional character, she'd be Robin Hood, because she has a strong sense of fairness, and is willing to stand up for people being bullied. Kim was already a strong writer before the group started, and has continued to write with real honesty and commitment.

Lewis Derosa – If Lewis was a car he'd be a Ferrari, because he's a quick thinker; if he was a video game he'd be Call of Duty, because it's not a game, it's a state of mind. He's got more energy than the national grid, and his classmates think he's a complete legend; he's also got the cheekiest grin in Cheney Plus. His poems are short, and to the point.

Mathew Rose – If Mathew was a car, he'd be . . . very happy indeed. And he'd almost certainly have a V8 engine. Because Mathew really, really loves cars – big cars – and motorbikes too; and it's fair to say that they feature very strongly in his poems. Mathew also has a real ability to tell a story, as his longer pieces show. Just be careful you don't disrespect Jeremy Clarkson . . .

Ryan Eeley – If Ryan was a superhero, he'd be Inspector Gadget, because he's always up to something; but if he was a colour, he'd be yellow, because he can be bright. To begin with Ryan's poems were never more six lines long, but his writing has grown in confidence, and his poem School Jumper shows both his creativity and his dry sense of humour.

Stacey Jennings – If Stacey was an animal she'd be a cat, because they sleep all day and can be in whenever they like. She likes spaghetti bolognese, chocolate gateau and the colour pink. She claims she's "loopy", but she's definitely much smarter than she lets on; and once she came out from Kimmie's shadow she started to show what she's capable of.

Tom Booth – If Tom was a household appliance he'd be a refrigerator – because he just loves to chill . . . Rarely seen without his iPod, he's a real music lover, and a one-man encyclopedia of song lyrics. When we were able to get his attention focused on the page he proved what a sharp mind he has, and he ended up producing some really clever pieces of writing.

Tyron Harries – If Tyron was a dog he'd be a pit bull, because he's feisty; if he was a PS3 game he'd be Grand Theft Auto, because he likes getting into trouble. We can always rely on Tyron to bring the conversation round to girls in a matter of seconds, but he's also been willing to take some real risks in his writing, and to reveal his more emotional side.

I'd also like to mention **Amare St Hilaire**, who wasn't a member of the group but who contributed a poem to the book; and **Vic Moore**, who took time out from keeping order in the classroom to have a go at writing himself – with very successful results!